JUN 0 7 2022

P9-DCV-628

In memory of Michael Stewart

Katherine Tegen Books is an imprint of HarperCollins Publishers.

Boogie Boogie, Y'all   Copyright © 2021 by C. G. Esperanza
All rights reserved. Manufactured in Italy.
No part of this book may be used or reproduced in any manner whatsoever without written permission
except in the case of brief quotations embodied in critical articles and reviews. For information address
HarperCollins Children's Books, a division of HarperCollins Publishers, 195 Broadway, New York, NY 10007.
www.harpercollinschildrens.com

Library of Congress Control Number: 2020941230
ISBN 978-0-06-297622-2

The artist used oils, acrylic, and Photoshop to create the digital illustrations for this book.
Typography by Rachel Zegar   21 22 23 24 25   RTLO   10 9 8 7 6 5 4 3 2 1   ❖   First Edition

By C. G. Esperanza

KT KATHERINE TEGEN BOOKS
An Imprint of HarperCollins Publishers

BOOGIE
BOOGIE,
Y'ALL.

The city BOOGIED all day.

Busy, **busy,** **busy,** till one kid stopped to say...

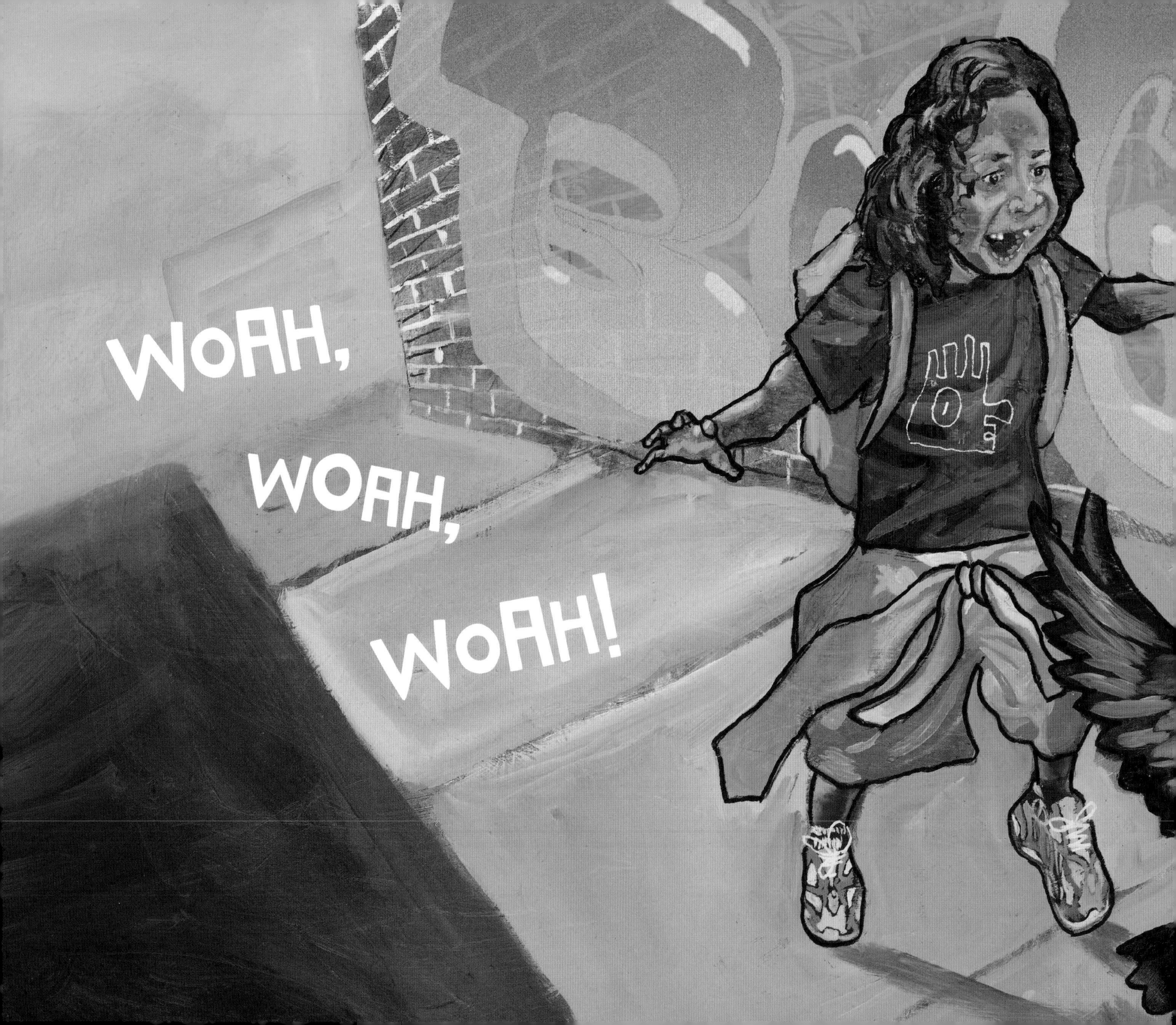

WOAH,
WOAH,
WOAH!

Look at the **ART** on the **WALL!**

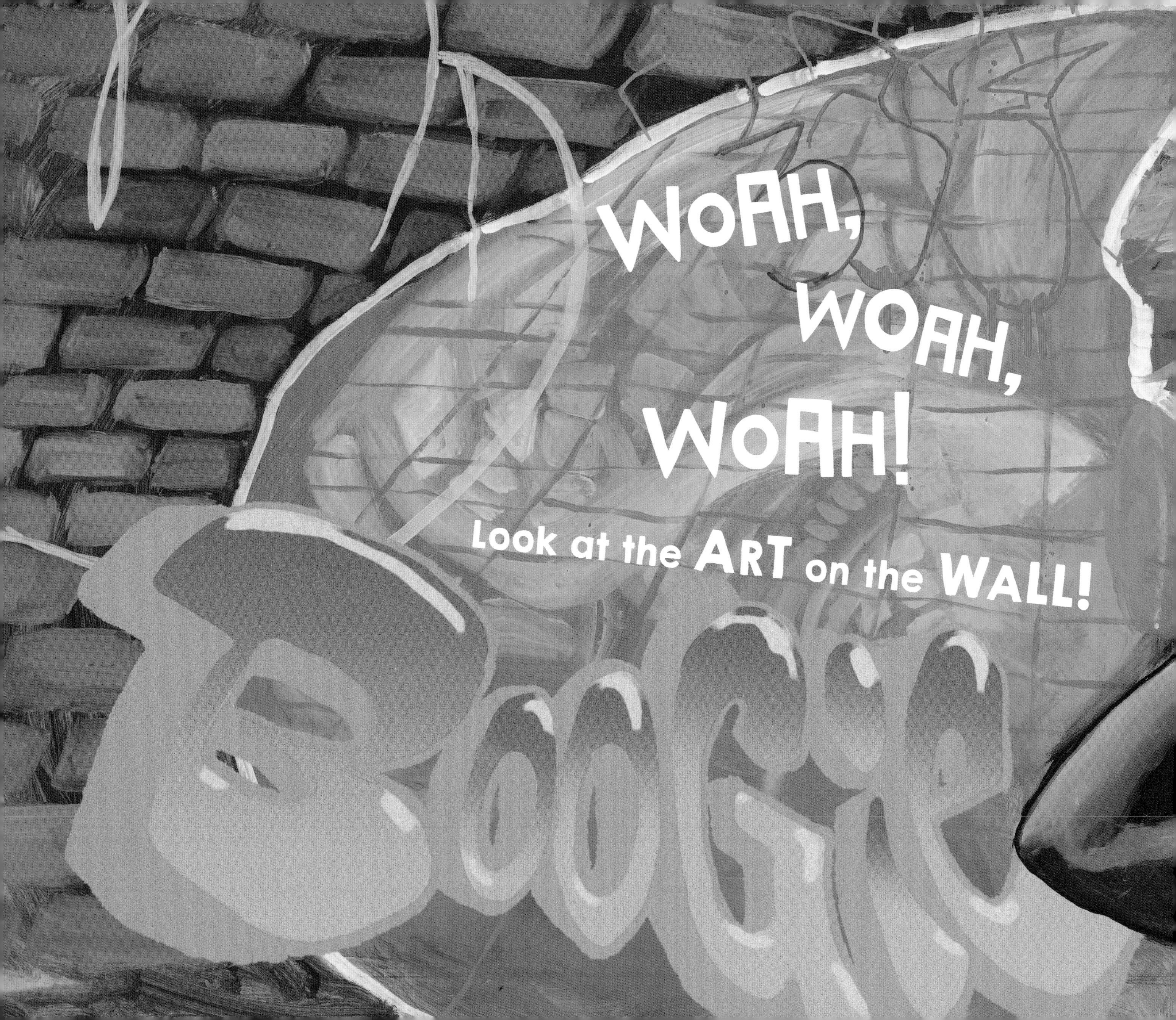

WOAH,
WOAH,
WOAH!

Look at the ART on the WALL!

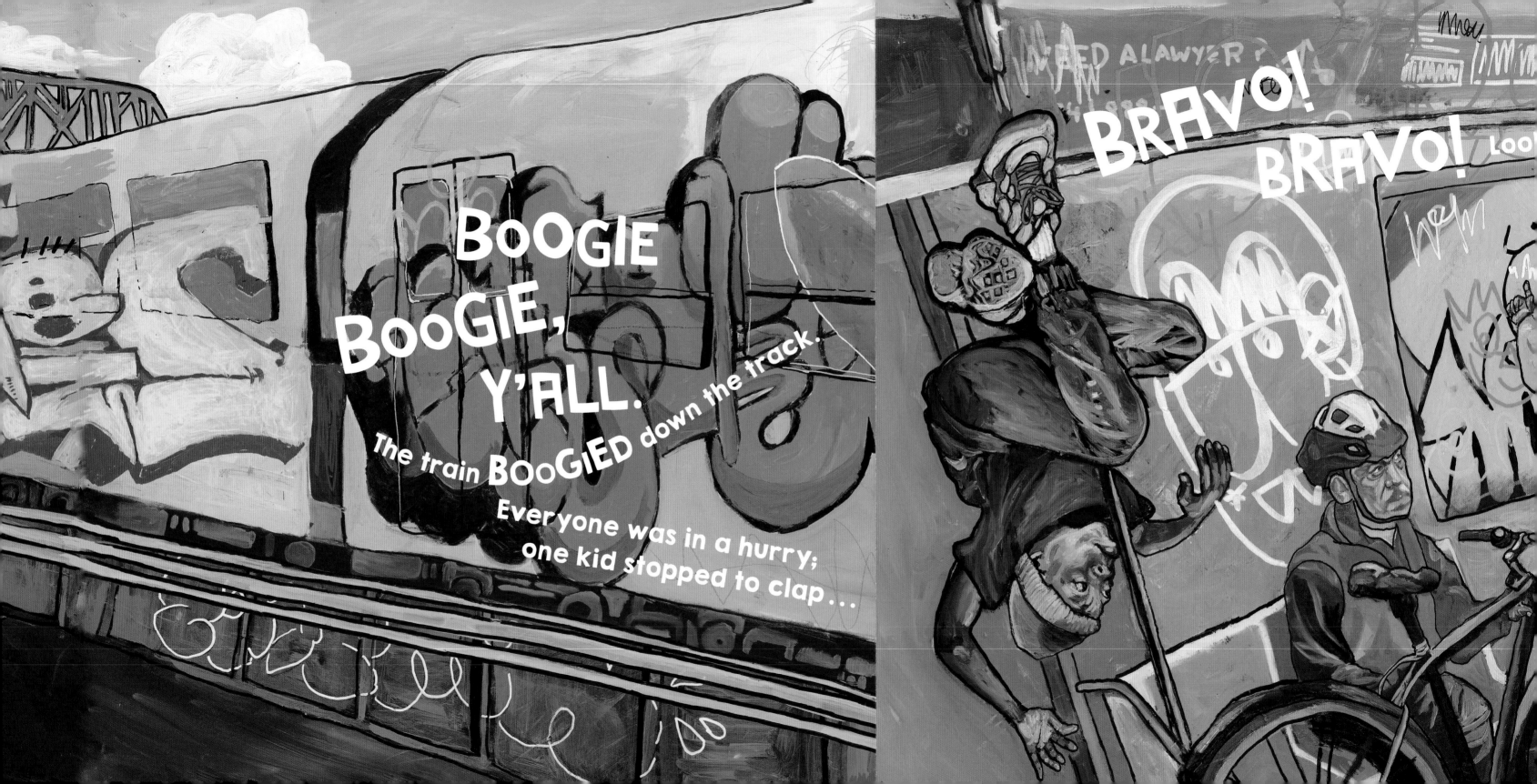

BoOGIE
BooGIE,
Y'ALL.

The train BOoGiEd down the track.

Everyone was in a hurry;
one kid stopped to clap...

BRAVo!

BRAVo! Loo

Yuck, gross, horrible.

Awful, yuck, awful.

Everyone else complained about the **ART** on the **TRAIN.**

BOOGIE BOOGIE, Y'ALL.

The kids BOOGIED in the park.

Jump, skip, hop.

One dog began to bark.

BoW!

WOW!

WOW!

Look at the **ART** in the **PARK!**

Look at the ART in the PARK!

Jump, skip, slide.

Hip to the hop.

No one cared at all about the **ART** in the **PARK!**

The Boogie Down Block Party **boogied** in the sun.

Up,

down,

all around,

the block was having fun!

"COCO, MANGO, CHERRY!"
yelled the man with icy treats,

while the break crew BOOGIED
to a BombaYo beat!

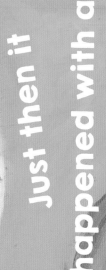

Just then it happened with a

the whole block was bubblin' and having a blast.

BOOM, ALAKAZOOM!

The art BOOGiED off the wall.

BOOM,
ALAKAZOOM!

The art BOOGIED off the wall!

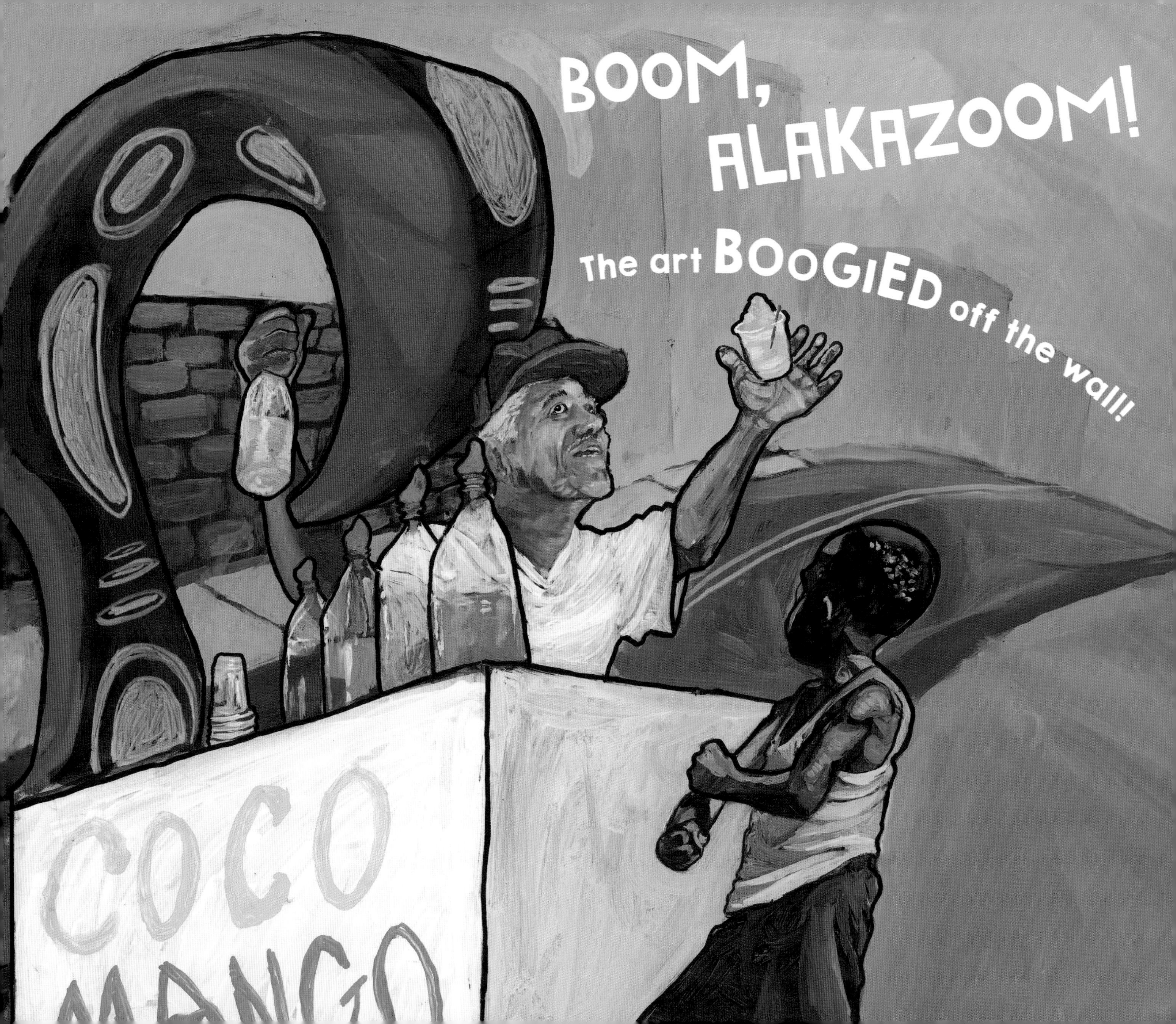

Everyone BOoGiED away.

a dog,

and cans of paint spray!

They shook the cans and sprayed.

You won't believe the **ART** they made!

BOOGIE BOOGIE, Y'ALL.

Bang a drum,
don't run!

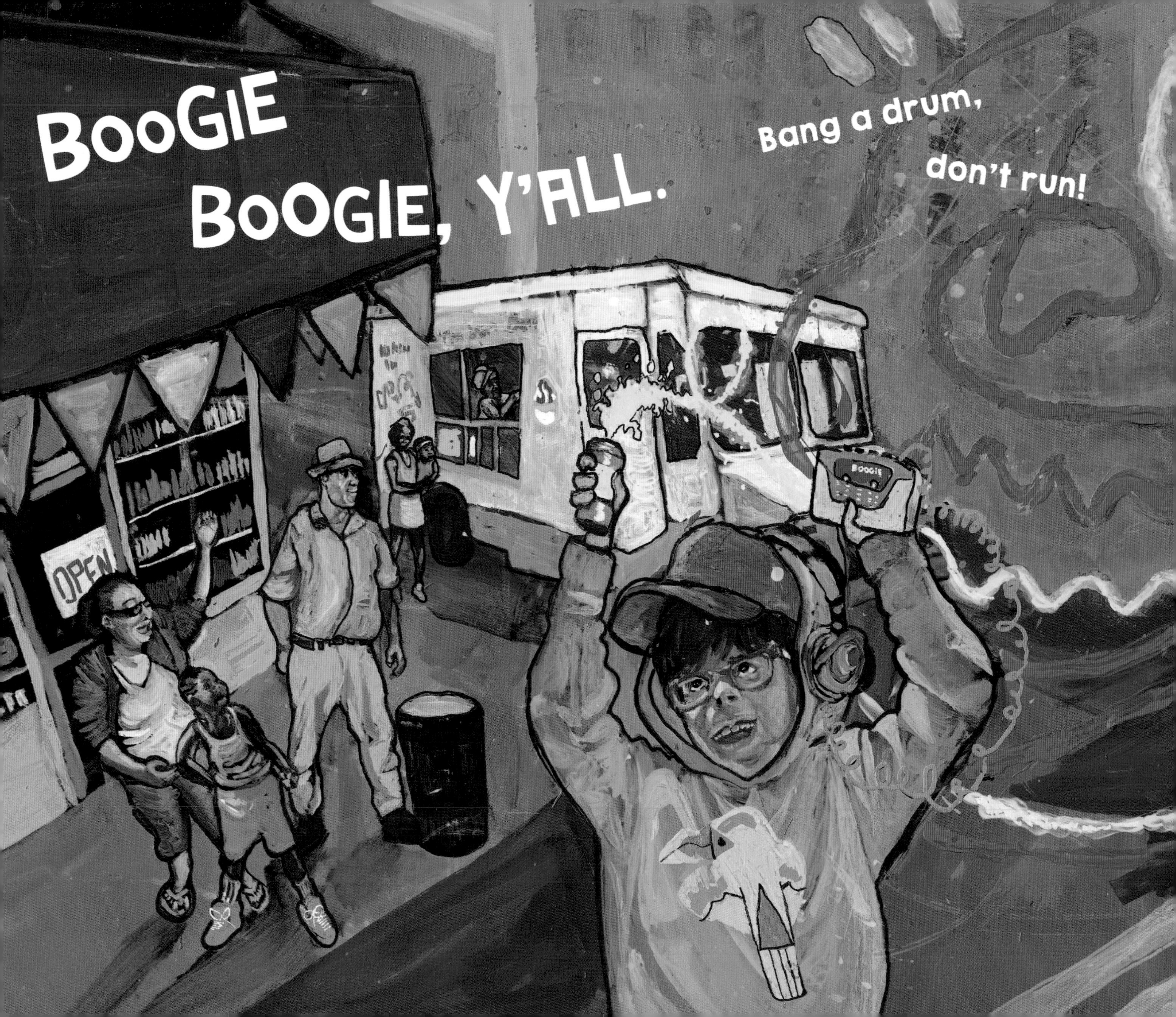

The art on the walls makes the block mad fun!

The block began to **BOOGiE**

till the block became the art . . .

or the art became the block . . .

I forget that part.

BOOGIE-BOOGIE, Y'ALL.

We BOOGIED down and had a ball.

And that's the tale of how the ART came off the WALL!